The Cup Final

JANET BURCHETT AND
SARA VOGLER

Illustrated by
Guy Parker-Rees

BLOOMSBURY
CHILDREN'S
BOOKS

For Simon and Robin Middleburgh

First published in Great Britain in 1998
Bloomsbury Publishing Plc, 38 Soho Square, London, W1V 5DF

Copyright © Text Janet Burchett and Sara Vogler 1998
Copyright © Illustrations Guy Parker-Rees 1998

The moral right of the author has been asserted
A CIP catalogue record of this book is available from the
British Library

ISBN 0 7475 3928 6 (hardback)
ISBN 0 7475 3851 4 (paperback)

Printed in England by Clays Ltd, St Ives plc

10 9 8 7 6

The Cup Final

OTHER TITLES IN THE SAME SERIES

Ghost Goalie
0 7475 3925 1 (hbk)
0 7475 3846 8 (pbk)

The coach has come down with chicken-pox and the
Tigers are desperate to win against Rockfield Rangers in
the final match of a knock-out competition. Can they
win? They might – when Billy gets very special help . . .

Save the Pitch
0 7475 3926 X (hbk)
0 7475 3847 6 (pbk)

The Tigers must win the last game of the season to go to
the top of the Junior Football league. But the pitch has
been invaded by workmen, and unless the Tigers get help
fast it looks like the game will be called off.

The Terrible Trainer
0 7475 3927 8 (hbk)
0 7475 3850 6 (pbk)

Mr Bawl is called in as substitute coach, but he is mean
and shouts a lot and makes the Tigers feel awful. How
can they get rid of him and get the ideal substitute who
will always ensure they win?

THE TIGERS

Mona (GK)

Terry   RICK   LISA   Blocker

Joe   ROB   Ellen   Kim

Bullseye   Billy Bright

Logo   Coach Mr. Bright

The Cup Final

Billy Bright and the Tigers
Football Team were in the final
of the UEFA Cup. If they won,
they would go into the record
books. The Under-Elevens
Football Association Cup had

never been won by nine-year-olds before.

The Tigers were on the Tottingham Town pitch. They were supposed to be warming-up but they weren't. They were standing round their coach, Billy's dad. Mr Bright had been reaching for a ball that had

gone over. His head was stuck in the railings. Billy and Rob pulled at Dad's trousers. He didn't budge.

'Ouch!' he yelled. 'Mind my ears.'

'Try wriggling your head, Mr Bright,' said Ellen.

'It hurts,' groaned Billy's dad.

'Bend the railings, Mr Bright,' suggested Bullseye.

'I'm not Superman,' moaned Mr Bright. 'This is a job for . . . the fire brigade.'

'Your mum's a fire officer, Blocker,' said Lisa. 'Is she on duty?'

'Yes,' said Blocker. 'I'll phone her. She'll be really

pleased. She thought she was
going to miss the match.'

Blocker went to find a
telephone.

'But how am I going to
coach you?' said Mr Bright.

His bottom was facing the
pitch.

'The fire brigade will get you
free soon,' said Billy.

'Billy'll coach us till then, Mr Bright,' said Kim.

'He's a good coach,' said Terry.

'When he gets going!' added Bullseye.

'Still got your book, Billy?' asked Mona the goalkeeper.

Whenever Billy's dad couldn't coach, Billy stepped in. The Tigers thought Billy and his coaching book were really good. They didn't know Billy's secret. Billy didn't have a book. He was helped by Springer Spannell – Tottingham Town's most famous goalkeeper. Everyone had heard of Springer but only Billy could see him. Springer Spannell was . . . a

SPRINGER SPANNELL
THE GREATEST

ghost! Billy wasn't allowed to tell anyone. It was in Springer's PhIFA rules.

The Tigers ran on to the pitch. The opposition had already arrived. They looked very big. Billy looked round for Springer. Springer always turned up when he was needed. But there was no sign of him yet.

'What's first?' asked Joe.

'Ummm,' said Billy.

He was a terrible coach on his own. He remembered something he'd heard on the telly.

'Squat thrusts, arm stretches, side bends,' he called. '. . . Or was it arm thrusts, side stretches and squat bends?'

Rob tried a couple of side thrusts and fell over. Lisa flung

both arms out at once and
knocked Ellen and Bullseye
flying. Terry did a squatting
arm bend. It hit Blocker on the
nose just as he arrived back
from the phone.

'That's a funny way to warm
up,' said a voice.

Billy turned. There was a

man sitting in the Mayor's seat.
He was wobbly round the
edges. Billy could see right
through him. It was like
looking through a banana jelly.

'Springer!' yelled Billy.

'Spring?' asked Blocker.

'Okay, Coach,' said Ellen.

The Tigers started springing

round the pitch. Rob sprang off to the toilet.

'Sorry I'm late, Billy,' said Springer. 'I had to iron my kit. Where's your dad this time?'

'Over there,' mumbled Billy, embarrassed. 'He's stuck.'

'Oh dear,' said Springer. 'Tell him to rub butter on his ears. Now let's get started. Who are you playing?'

'Nutfield Road,' said Billy.

'The Nutters!' gasped Springer. 'We'll have to keep an eye on them.'

'Why?'

'I've seen them play, lad,' said Springer. 'They're a nasty side. They're always up to something.'

He pointed at Mr Bright.
Someone had stuck a note on
his bottom.

Billy ran and tore the note
off.

'Have the fire brigade arrived
yet?' asked Dad. 'My neck
hurts.'

'Won't be long,' said Billy.

*

The crowd started waving their scarves. The Mayor took his seat. The UEFA cup stood gleaming in front of him. The referee called the teams over. Close up, the Nutters looked even bigger. They wore a dirty

grey and black kit. The Tigers
suddenly felt very small.

'The Nutters don't play fair,'
said Springer. 'Tell the team to
watch out for dirty tricks.'

Billy told the Tigers in a
whisper. He didn't want the
Nutters to hear. The teams got
into position. The referee tossed
a coin. The Tigers won. They
chose the town hall end.

It would be the Nutters' kick-off.

'Where's Rob?' shouted Blocker.

The Tigers looked round anxiously.

'Let's get on with it,' growled the Nutters' captain. 'If he's not here – tough!'

'Well . . .' said the referee.

Even *he* looked scared of the Nutters.

'I'll go and find him,' said Billy.

But as he ran to look, the match started. There were only nine Tigers on the pitch!

Billy started searching round.

'Have you seen Rob anywhere?' he asked Dad.

'All I can see is this ants' nest,' said Dad, gloomily. 'Have the fire brigade arrived yet? My back hurts.'

'Won't be long,' said Billy.

Then he heard a shout.

'Help! I'm stuck in the toilet!'

Billy ran and unlocked the toilet door. Rob tumbled out.

'The Nutters shut me in,' he wailed.

'Quick!' said Billy. 'The match has started.'

And, at that moment, they heard the roar of the crowd. Someone had scored. Billy and

Rob raced back on to the field.

'Where've you been?' demanded Ellen.

'We're one-nil down,' said Rick.

'We're going to lose!' groaned Bullseye.

'No we're not,' said Billy. 'We're all here now.'

But then Billy realised he couldn't see Springer. He had

no time to find him. It was the
Tigers' kick-off. Billy passed to
Kim but she was knocked
flying by a late challenge. The
Nutters had possession. They
headed for the goal. They
looked mean and hard. The

28

Tigers' defence wanted to run away. Billy knew he should be shouting instructions. He needed Springer's help and he needed it now.

And then Billy saw Springer. Springer was standing on the Mayor's head.

'What are you doing?'
shouted Billy.

'Shaking with fright,' wailed
Blocker.

'Not you, Blocker,' sighed
Billy.

'Looking for Rob,' called
Springer.

'Rob's here!' shouted Billy.

'Wish I wasn't,' said Rob.

Springer suddenly pointed at
the Tigers' goal.

'What's the matter with
Mona?' he shouted.

Mona seemed to be dancing
in the goal-mouth. She was
twitching and jerking. She
didn't notice the Nutters coming
towards her. She didn't see the

ball hit the back of the net. The
Nutters were two-nil up. But
Mona just kept jigging about.

'Goalkeeping wasn't like that
in my day,' said Springer,
climbing down the Mayor.

'What's the matter, Mona?' shouted Billy.

'It's my hands,' sobbed Mona. 'They're itching. They're driving me mad!'

'They've used itching powder,' said Springer crossly.

'Better get those gloves off
her.'

Billy took Mona off the
pitch.

'What are we going to do
without Mona?' Billy asked
Springer.

'Don't ask me,' said Terry.

'You're the coach,' said
Lisa.

'Someone's got to go in
goal,' said Springer.

'Someone's got to go in
goal,' said Billy.

'Not me!' shouted the other

nine Tigers together.

'Looks like it's you, lad,' said Springer.

'I can't go in goal!' wailed Billy.

'Yes you can!' shouted the other nine Tigers together.

Billy stood in the goalmouth. He could feel his knees

chattering teeth →

knocking together. Springer stood by the post.

'It's no good,' hissed Billy. 'I'm not a goalkeeper.'

The Nutters heard him. They laughed.

'Don't worry,' said Springer. 'I'll coach you.'

'I wish you'd play instead of me,' said Billy.

'Sorry lad,' said Springer, shaking his head. 'PhIFA rule number thirteen. *A ghost coach – that's me – cannot come on as a substitute. If he does he gets the sack –* I disappear.'

There was nothing for it. Billy couldn't let the team down.

'Remember, lad,' said

Springer. 'Goalkeepers are not there just to stop shots. You've got to be ready to launch a counter-attack.'

'I'll be lucky to touch the ball,' wailed Billy.

'Listen to me,' said Springer firmly. 'Keep on your toes, ready to move. Don't take your

eyes off the ball. You can do it, lad.'

The play was coming Billy's way. He could hear the Nutters jeering at him.

'Ignore them,' said Springer. 'Watch out for that striker. Tell Blocker to tackle.'

'Tackle him, Blocker!'

shouted Billy desperately. 'Er
. . . Lisa? . . . Rick? . . . Terry?
. . . Someone!'

But the Tigers' defenders
were cowering. The Nutters
broke through easily.

'It's up to you, lad,' said
Springer. 'Stop shaking.
Narrow the angle . . . that's it
. . . he's got it on the left foot
. . . dive to your right!'

Billy closed his eyes and
dived. There was a roar from
the crowd. The Nutters must
have scored again. Billy opened
his eyes. He wished he hadn't.
There were boots rushing
towards him. Then someone
patted him on the back.

'Well done, Billy!'

'You're a star!'

'Good work, lad.'

Billy realised he was clutching the ball! Somehow he had saved the goal.

Billy got ready to kick the ball. The Nutters weren't in a hurry to get back up the field.

'He was lucky,' snarled the striker.

'He won't kick it far,' said a defender.

'He's too weedy!' shouted the goalkeeper.

'We'll boot it straight back in the net,' sneered the Nutters' captain.

'Lean into it,' Springer told

Billy. 'Take your foot as far
back as you can. That'll give it
power. Watch the ball all the
time. Off you go.'

Billy kicked the ball with all his
might. It sailed over the heads

of the Tigers. It sailed over the
heads of the Nutters. It sailed
straight towards the Nutters'
goal. The Nutters' goalie had
come forwards to jeer at Billy.
The ball sailed over his head,
bounced four times and came to

rest just over the goal-line. Billy had scored from a goalkeeper's punt! It was two-one. The Tigers were in with a chance.

The whistle blew for half-time. Billy's dad was still stuck. But the fire brigade had arrived at last.

Billy and the Tigers huddled round. They knew the Nutters would want their revenge in the second half. And they weren't looking forward to it. The Tigers bit nervously into their half-time oranges. Springer began his team talk. But Billy wasn't listening. He had begun to sneeze and he couldn't stop.

'Bless you!' said Springer.

Then Blocker sneezed. And

Lisa. And Joe. And soon all the Tigers were sneezing their heads off.

'I think . . . a-tishoo . . . we've all got a cold,' sniffed Bullseye.

'I think we're allergic to the Nutters!' wheezed Rick.

'I think there's something wrong with . . . atchoo . . . these oranges!' gasped Kim.

'Quick!' shouted Springer.
'Throw them away. The Nutters
have put . . . wa-a-choo
. . . pepper on them!'

'Throw them away!'
spluttered Billy. 'The Nutters
have put . . . wa-a-choo . . .
pepper on them!'

The Nutters hadn't waited for the second half to get their revenge.

'Let's tell the referee,' sniffed Ellen.

'We can't prove anything,' said Rick.

The Tigers shuffled on to the pitch. Mona ran up. She was ready to go back in goal.

'I missed my half-time orange,' she complained.

'You were lucky,' snuffled Blocker.

It was the Tigers' kick off but their eyes were streaming. Bullseye thought he was passing to Billy but the ball went straight to the Nutters'

captain. She began a forwards run. Lisa ran up to challenge. She missed completely and collided with Terry. Blocker could see someone charging

towards him. He did a brilliant sliding tackle. Well, it would have been a brilliant sliding tackle . . . if it hadn't been on the referee!

'Sorry, Ref,' he quavered.

He waited to be sent off. But
the referee had other things on
his mind. There was a pile-up in
the Tigers' goalmouth. At the

bottom of the heap was the Nutters' captain.

'What's going on?' shouted the referee.

The referee blew his whistle. The Tigers blew their noses. The referee pointed to the penalty spot. The Nutters' captain placed the ball on the penalty spot.

'Tell Mona to sway to the right but dive to the left,' shouted Springer.'

Billy whispered to Mona. The players cleared the penalty area. Mona crouched ready. The crowd was silent. The Nutters' captain ran at the ball. She saw Mona sway to the right. So she hammered the ball

towards the left-hand corner of
the net. The Nutters started
cheering. It had to be a goal.

*

But Mona was ready. She made
a tremendous dive
to the left.

She hit the ground, the ball safe
in her hands. The Tigers
cheered. Springer swung on the
goalpost in excitement.

'What a save!' yelled the
crowd.

'That was just like Springer
Spannell!' yelled Lisa's
grandad.

'Ti-gers!' yelled the fire
brigade.

*

56

The fire officers had managed to undo a section of the fence. They turned Dad and his railings round so he could see the action. Well, he would have seen the action if his head hadn't been stuck. As it was, he could only see the corner flag.

'Don't you worry, Mr
Bright,' said Blocker's mum,
picking up the crowbar. 'We'll
have you out in a jiffy. Wait a
minute . . . my boy's got the
ball. Did you see that? What a
pass! Now it's Joe . . . on to
Bullseye. To Kim . . . and over
to Billy. Mind that defender . . .
it's okay, he's feinted round her.

He's coming up to the goal!
Can he do it?'

The crowd roared.

'What's going on?' wailed
Dad.

'Billy's scored!' shrieked
Blocker's mum, waving her
crowbar.

'Two-all!' yelled the fire
brigade.

'Good play,' said Springer. 'You've shown them. You don't have to cheat to win.'

'We haven't won yet,' panted Billy.

'Get back out there then,' said Springer. 'Go for your hat-trick.'

The Nutters were looking tired. They were a mean, hard side but they weren't fit. The Tigers

soon got possession. Rick
passed to Lisa who flicked the
ball on to Terry. Blocker took
it from him and ran up the
wing. Then it was Joe. He
back-heeled it to Kim. She
pushed it forwards to Rob who
lobbed it over to Ellen. She
found Bullseye. The Nutters ran
backwards and forwards but

they couldn't keep up. Billy had
plenty of space. Bullseye
chipped the ball to him. Then
the Nutters' captain came
lumbering over. She had an
ugly look on her face. She leapt
at Billy in a high, vicious
tackle. But at the last minute,
Billy swerved. The Nutters'

captain flew past him and
thumped heavily on to the
pitch.

Now it was just Billy and the
goalkeeper. Billy knew he had
to score. Time was running out.
He dribbled to the right,
swayed to the left and watched
the goalie dive. Then he punted
the ball right into the centre of
the net.

The final whistle blew. Billy
Bright had got his hat-trick.
And the Tigers had won the
UEFA Cup.

OTHER YOUNG FICTION SERIES

CRAZY GANG:

"Og Fo" says the Space Bug 0 7475 3929 4 (hbk) /3562 0 (pbk)
"Do I Look Funny to You?" 0 7475 3930 8 (hbk) /3561 2 (pbk)
Pets Just Want to Have Fun 0 7475 3931 6 (hbk) /3560 4 (pbk)
"I Don't Like Space Glop" 0 7475 3932 4 (hbk) /3563 9 (pbk)

Enjoy the zany, mad-cap world of Max and Pat, and their
space friends Jazz and Zug Zug, in these fun-filled books.
When Pat the dog and Zug Zug the space bug meet, they
just want to have fun – but they can't help causing trouble!
Join Max and Jazz trying to keep an eye on their pets, and
having a crazy time along the way!

BEST PETS:

Timmy and Tiger 0 7475 3878 6 (hbk) /3564 7 (pbk)
Gita and Goldie 0 7475 3879 4 (hbk) /3656 5 (pbk)
Becky and Beauty 0 7475 3880 8 (hbk) /3566 3 (pbk)
Paul and Percy 0 7475 3881 6 (hbk) /3567 1 (pbk)

Your pet can be your best friend. Your pet will be loyal to
you, and look out for you. Sometimes your pet can even
save you from danger . . . In these heartwarming stories,
Tiger the cat, Goldie the dog, Beauty the pony and Percy
the parrot, prove that they really are best pets!

Chapter One

"Hurry up!" cried Mum. "Breakfast is ready!"

Charlie opened his money box and tipped the contents onto his bedroom carpet.

"COMING!" he yelled.

Mike poked his head round the door.

"Wow!" he gasped.

"Go away!" Charlie growled.

Mike made a grab at the coins and picked up a handful.

"Give that back, or else! I've been saving to buy Mum's birthday present. There's a brilliant shop at Farm Park, and today we're going there on our school outing."

Charlie threw his slipper at Mike, but it hit Sheeba the cat. Sheeba shot under the bed and poked her nose out, twitching her whiskers angrily. Mike laughed, so Charlie attacked him with the other slipper.

"OUCH! OUCH!" he yelled.

Dad stormed in and Mike dropped the money on the floor.

"Will you two stop this noise and come downstairs at once."

Mike followed him out with

Sheeba at his heels. He slid down the banisters and landed with a bump at the bottom.

Charlie gathered up his money and stuffed it into an old sock. Tying the top with string, he pushed it into his back trouser pocket.

"BOTHER!" he muttered. "The string's too long. Oh well, it won't matter."

In the kitchen, Josie was feeding her doll with cornflakes. The milk ran down the doll's body and onto the floor, where Sheeba was busily lapping the puddle.

"About time, Charlie!" grumbled Mum. "Eat your cereal quickly. We don't want to miss the coach from school to Farm Park."

"The road works are still holding up the traffic," remarked Dad. "I was late for work yesterday."

"Where's my picnic lunch?" asked Charlie.

"It's in your school bag," replied Mum. "Sheeba has been sniffing round it already. I've made your favourite sardine sandwiches."

"GREAT!" Charlie grinned. "Thanks, Mum."

"Here's fifty p. for a can of coke," added Dad.

"Wish I were going," grumbled Mike. "Lucky thing!"

They scrambled into the car and soon joined the long queue of traffic.

"That's Willie Smith in front!" remarked Charlie. "He's sitting in

4

the back of the car with their smelly
labrador dog." The dog stared
dolefully out of the window.

"Look at it now!" laughed Mum.
"Willie has put his school cap on the
poor dog's head. It does look a
scream!"

The cars began to crawl along.
Mum followed with a jerk and the
car lurched to one side.

"I can't steer properly!" she protested. "I do believe we've a puncture!"

Charlie's stomach turned a somersault as she ground to a halt.

"I'll miss the coach!" he moaned when all the cars in front moved away.

"And we're holding up everybody else!" shouted Mike.

Suddenly a police car drew up alongside.

"What's the trouble?" asked the policeman.

"It's a puncture!" Mum explained, looking flustered. "And my son Charlie will miss the coach. He's going on a school trip."

"We'll have to do something about

6

that!" the policeman decided, turning to his companion.

"Hop out, Jones! Cope with the car and move the traffic on. But first of all get Charlie in the back and I'll take him to school."

Charlie found himself sitting in the back of the police car overtaking everything.'

"Hold tight! We'll get you there in no time!"

"That's our coach!" Charlie cried. "It's moving off."

"Here we go!" grinned the policeman. "We'll put the siren on and see if we can catch it!"

ZOOM! SWISH! BRRRRRUMM! The police car, siren screaming, overtook the coach as it slowed to a standstill.

"Out you get, Charlie!" he cried.

Charlie, red-faced but feeling rather important, followed the policeman to the coach. Bert, the driver, looked flustered.

"Here's one that nearly got left behind!" the policeman laughed. "I'll get back to see if his mum's been rescued. She's had a puncture."

"Hop up!" grinned Bert. He hauled Charlie inside to cheers and claps from all the others, including Mr Taylor and Mr Kerry.

"Cor!" gasped Titch. "Lucky thing. Going in a police car!"

"Come here, Charlie!" Joe pleaded. "I've saved you a seat."

"You'd better tell us all about it

8

before you sit down," decided Bert.
"Speak through this microphone,
then we'll be able to hear you."

Charlie found his voice sounded
quite different with the microphone,
but halfway through his story he
suddenly stopped.

"OH NO!" he cried. "I've left my school bag in the police car and my sandwiches are inside."

There was a howl of sympathy from all his friends.

"You can have some of mine!" shouted Jake. "I've plenty."

"AND MINE!" chorused Tony, Mac and Dave.

Bert switched off the microphone and there was a moment's silence.

"Broadcast finished for today," Mr Kerry announced. "We'll be at Farm Park very soon."

Charlie sat down with a bump next to Joe and in no time at all the coach rattled into Farm Park.

Chapter Two

"ALL OUT!" shouted Mr Taylor.

"Don't forget your picnic," added Mr Kerry. "We'll be paying a visit to the shop before we eat so you can buy drinks there, and anything else you'd like."

Charlie felt in his pockets to make sure his money was safe. Thank goodness he'd only left his sandwiches behind.

"We'll keep together as far as we can. A farm worker is joining us to show us round. His name is Pete. After our picnic you can wander about on your own."

They clambered out of the coach and clustered round the first pen. Geese, ducks and hens waddled everywhere. The air rang with their gobbling, clucking, honking cries.

"The board above tells you all about the animal," said Mr Taylor. "This runt end pig was the last of a litter of thirteen. He's called after Houdini who was a magician and could escape from anywhere. This little chap is just the same!"

"Phew! What a stink!" complained Titch.

"These are even smellier!"
laughed Joe as they moved on to the
next pen.

Mr Kerry looked up at the board.

"This is Mick, the angora goat,"
he read. "His woolly coat makes
wonderfully warm jerseys, and he's
very cheeky!"

Mick sprang on to the top rung of
the fence and Dave tickled him under
the chin.

"Hey up!" he cried. "He's trying
to eat *me* now!"

"Look out, Charlie!" laughed
Titch. "That duck has taken a liking
to you."

"Here's Pete come to help us,"
said Mr Kerry. "This duck is
following Charlie everywhere. Does it
follow other people too?"

15

"It's an Indian runner duck," explained Pete. "A student reared it from an egg then gave it to the Farm Park. Some of the animals are so tame they roam free and follow anyone."

"This calf's sucking my fingers!" Trevor shouted.

"His mother died when he was born, and he's very hungry. Would you like to give him a bottle of special milk, Charlie?"

Everybody watched as the calf
tugged greedily at the teat.

"He's nearly pulling me over!"
cried Charlie delightedly.

Bill and Titch gave the hens pans
of meal and water.

"Look here!" cried Bill. "This hen
has a silky coat and feathers right
down to her feet."

"There's another the same,
pecking in the corner," pointed Pete.

"They're white cochins and called Polly and Molly."

There were barn owls and tawny owls, blind pheasants, a grouse with a broken wing, and other injured birds.

"They were rescued and brought here," explained Pete. "They would have died in the wild. Some animals need protection. That's why they're kept in pens instead of roaming freely in the fields."

"Look at this whopper!" exclaimed Titch. "A black Norfolk turkey. It's very bad-tempered and is called El Cid!"

"You'll see more of the tougher animals in the fields," announced Mr Taylor. "But we'll visit the shop first."

Charlie, Joe and Titch inspected the shelves. There were books about animals, crayons, pen-knives, china animals, games, cricket bats and balls.

"I'm buying Mum's birthday present," explained Charlie. "Wow! Look at this super police car!"

"My mum wouldn't want that," decided Joe.

"Nor mine," agreed Titch.

Charlie's heart sank. He knew his mum wouldn't either.

He reached for a china rabbit and studied it carefully.

"I'll have this," he gulped. "She likes rabbits."

"Get a move on!" Mr Taylor

snapped. "You three are last!"

The boys grabbed a tin of coke and Joe and Titch paid at the till.

"I'll wrap the rabbit in special paper and you can collect it later," the girl said to Charlie. "That'll be three pounds, fifty."

He tipped some of the coins out of the sock and, clutching his tin of coke, rushed out to join the others.

Everybody shared their food with Charlie. The tame animals trotted about the yard nipping under the tables to gobble up the crumbs.

"I'm full to bursting!" Charlie groaned. "And I'll have my sardine sandwiches to eat when I get home."

"HEY!" cried Dave. "Who's pinched my last sandwich?"

They looked round to see a goat trotting away with the sandwich hanging out of his mouth.

"STOP! THIEF!" shouted Charlie, leaping to his feet to corner the goat. The Indian duck followed Charlie, tugging at the string which was hanging out from his back pocket.

"LOOK OUT, CHARLIE!"
yelled Titch. "The duck's just run off
with your sock full of money."

"HELP!" Charlie cried, chasing
after the duck.

The duck nipped between troughs,
waddled over the soggy grass by the
pond and through the prickly bushes.

"COME BACK!" shrieked
Charlie. His trainers squelched with
water.

There was a roar of laughter as Mr Kerry focused his video camera on the scene.

"What a great film show this will make!" he predicted.

The goat dropped the sandwich and disappeared. The duck dropped the sock to gobble up the sandwich, then waddled away.

"Phew!" gasped Charlie as he grabbed the sock. "That was a near disaster!"

"Time to explore the fields!" announced Mr Taylor. "But when you hear my whistle, come back straight away."

"HURRAH!" they shouted. "HERE WE GO!"

Chapter Three

Pete led the way to the first field and introduced them to Topsy, a Shetland pony.

"You need grooming, my beauty," said Pete.

He handed Titch a brush and he soon got busy.

"You can brush harder than that," advised Pete. "Topsy won't mind at all."

They took turns to help and then sat on Topsy for a ride.

"It's a bit tickly!" laughed Joe. "But it's great."

Topsy loved this and enjoyed the gentle pats and fuss she got from them all.

"I have to harness the big Shire horse now," said Pete. "It sometimes

works in the field and can pull a
weight of five tonnes."

"Phew!" they gasped.

"His name's Brigadier and he's
shiny black with feathered legs and
white stockings. Look out for him on
your way back. I'll leave you to
wander round on your own now."

There were lots of paddocks; some where sheep grazed lazily, others where Jersey cows, with their creamy-coloured coats, swished their long tails to ward off the flies. There were red deer, always on the alert but safe in their high fenced enclosures.

"What's in that field?" Jason pointed. "I'm a bit bored."

Jason climbed over the fence. A herd of bullocks was grazing peacefully under an old oak tree in the corner.

"Come on!" he shouted. "I've brought my football and we can have a game!"

Charlie, Jake, Joe, Bill, Titch and Jason wasted no time. They were soon roaring down the field weaving in and out, dribbling the ball, passing to each other and kicking for goal.

"Hey up!" warned Bill suddenly. "Here's trouble!"

Bob, Dave and Terry, bullies from the rival gang in their class, appeared from nowhere. Bob snatched the ball from Titch and gave it an almighty kick into the bullocks.

"Keep cool and don't move!" advised Jake. "Let's see what happens."

"AFTER IT!" yelled Bob.

Dave and Terry hurtled after Bob in the chase for the ball, but as they approached, the startled bullocks turned on the three boys and charged.

"HELP! HELP!" they screamed, turning tail and running for their lives.

"Look at the three scaredy cats scrambling over the fence!" cried Charlie. "Serves them right!"

"There's the whistle," said Jason. "I'll collect the ball then race you to the coach!"

"It's further than I thought," panted Jake.

They leant against a fence to catch their breath, then Jason kicked the ball with a thwack and it went flying into another field.

"Now look what you've done!" yelled Charlie. "COME ON!"

This field was full of thistles and a donkey was busily nudging their ball.

"Cheeky thing!" said Titch as he gleefully snatched it away.

The donkey looked affronted. It pawed the ground with a hoof and bucked its hind legs.

"LOOK OUT, CHARLIE!" yelled Joe.

Charlie went down with a bang as the donkey butted him.

"OUCH!" he cried. He sprang to his feet and joining in the laughter rubbed his behind.

"There's the whistle again!" cried Titch. "We'll catch it if we don't get back straight away."

They tumbled into the coach panting furiously, and bumped down on the seats. Mr Kerry glared at them as Bert revved the engine.

"Stop!" shouted Charlie. "I've forgotten Mum's present."

Before Mr Kerry could say a word Charlie was out of the coach and racing into the shop.

"I thought you'd gone without your rabbit, Charlie!" exclaimed the girl.

"I hope they wait for me," he

trembled. He clutched the parcel and ran.

To Charlie's relief Mr Kerry was waiting on the coach steps.

"Come on Charlie!" he grinned. "You nearly got left behind!"

They were having a sing song on the way back when Terry raised his voice above the din.

"Please, Mr Kerry," he shouted. "Dave has gone a green colour and I

don't think he's very well."

"Oh dear!" groaned Mr Kerry. "Take deep breaths, Dave, and swallow hard."

"Serves him right for ganging up on us in the field with Bob and Terry," whispered Jason to Jake. "He was scared to death when those bullocks chased them."

"Yes," laughed Jake. "That'll teach him!"

"Oooh, I feel terrible," Dave moaned.

"You'll be OK," Mr Kerry said firmly. "We're nearly back now, thank goodness."

When Charlie got home from school, the family had already started their tea. He rushed upstairs

and hid Mum's present under the
loose floorboard in his bedroom.

"Rabbits like being underground,"
he muttered. Then he slid down the
bannisters and rushed into the
kitchen.

"I've had a great time!" he cried.

"Fancy riding in a police car!"
Dad said. "Mum's told me all about
it."

"The animals were super and a

donkey butted my bottom and Dave nearly threw up in the coach," gabbled Charlie.

"Steady on, steady on!" laughed Mum. "By the way, the nice policeman returned your school bag which you left in the car."

Charlie sat down with a bump at the table.

"Great! I can eat my sardine sandwiches now," he grinned.

"Well – er, I'm afraid not." Mum paused. "You see, the policeman and Jones looked really hungry whilst we were waiting for the garage man to fix the tyre, so I gave them your sandwiches."

"WHAT?" Charlie exclaimed.

"We're all having beans on toast," Mum said firmly.

Charlie thought for a moment.

"Well! If it hadn't been for the policeman, I couldn't have gone on the outing."

"That's right," agreed Mum. "Anyway, he asked me to give you this bag. It's a present for you because he ate your sandwiches!"

"COR!" said Charlie. He delved
into the bag and pulled out a box. "I
wonder what it is?"

He opened it quickly and gasped.

"It's a police car!" cried Charlie. "Just like the one I saw in the Farm Park shop. I shall write and thank him."

That night, Charlie placed the car carefully on his bedside table as Mum came into the room.

"Good night, Charlie," she said. "What an exciting day!"

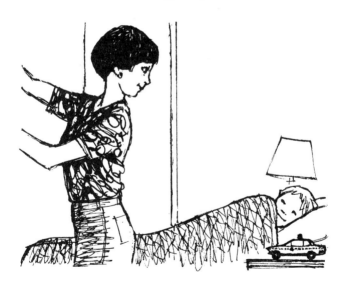

"The ride in the police car was the best part of all!" he announced sleepily. "And I've bought you a lovely present. I've hidden it, but you can't look for it until tomorrow when it's your birthday."

Then he turned on his side and fell fast asleep.